*B*eautiful **Amy March,** the youngest March sister, is a talented artist. Everyone praises her lifelike portraits. The one person she can't draw is herself. So when a photographer's studio opens in town, Amy is thrilled. Now her pretty curls and piercing eyes can be captured forever in a photograph. A photograph costs quite a bit of money — more than Amy has, and more than her parents can give her. Amy thinks of a clever way to come up with the money . . . and soon she has enough. But Amy decides to spend her savings on a gift for her father — a gift that will warm his heart when he's far away from home, and that ultimately brings Amy an unexpected gift in return.

# PORTRAITS
## of LITTLE WOMEN

*Amy's Story*

Don't miss any of the
Portraits of Little Women

# PORTRAITS
## of LITTLE WOMEN
# *Amy's Story*

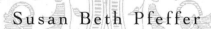

Susan Beth Pfeffer

DELACORTE PRESS

Published by
Delacorte Press
Bantam Doubleday Dell Publishing Group, Inc.
1540 Broadway
New York, New York 10036

**Library of Congress Cataloging-in-Publication Data**
Pfeffer, Susan Beth.
Portraits of Little Women, Amy's story/Susan Beth Pfeffer.
p.    cm.
Based on characters found in Louisa May Alcott's Little Women.
Summary: Because she desperately wants to have her picture taken,
ten-year-old Amy finds a way to accumulate the necessary five dollars
but then decides to spend it in another way.
ISBN 0-385-32529-0
[1. Photography — Fiction.   2. Generosity — Fiction.   3. Family life —
Fiction.]   I. Alcott, Louisa May, 1832–1888. Little Women.   II. Title.
III. Title: Amy's story.
PZ7.P44855Pk      1997
[Fic] — dc21                                                              97-6137
                                                                            CIP
                                                                            AC

The text of this book is set in 13-point Cochin.

Cover and text design by Patrice Sheridan
Cover illustration copyright © 1997 by Lori Earley
Text illustrations copyright © 1997 by Marcy Ramsey
Activities illustrations copyright © 1997 by Laura Maestro

Manufactured in the United States of America

November 1997

10   9   8   7   6   5   4   3   2   1

BVG

FOR GEORGIE STEINMAN

# PORTRAITS
## of LITTLE WOMEN

# Amy's Story

# CHAPTER 1

"What do you want most in the world, Amy?" Jo March asked her youngest sister.

It was a Saturday afternoon in April. There was a scent of springtime in the air, but it was too cold for Amy and her sisters, Meg, Jo, and Beth, to be playing outside. Instead they were in the parlor. Their parents were visiting their friends the Emersons.

Amy could recall a time when she and her sisters were regarded as too young to be left alone. But now Meg was fifteen, Jo fourteen, Beth twelve, and Amy almost eleven.

"Why do you want to know?" Amy asked.

"I was just wondering," Jo replied. "I know what I want the most: to be a famous writer. And Meg wants a husband and babies. Am I right, Meg?"

"I would like a husband and babies," Meg said with a smile. "But not for another week or two, thank you. Right now what I'd like more than anything is a new dress. One I could wear to parties and not be ashamed of."

"You have nothing to be ashamed of," Beth said. "You dress beautifully, Meg."

Meg sighed. "Not compared to the girls I know. Anyway, that's what I want. A pretty new party dress."

"I want all of us to be happy," said Beth. "And some new sheet music. And a really fine piano. And a new head for my doll. Her headless body looks so sad."

"That's quite a list," Jo said. "Now, Amy, what's your pleasure?"

"A truly aristocratic nose," Amy replied.

2

"You ought to know, Jo, since it's your fault I don't have one."

"Will you never let me forget?" Jo said. "I didn't mean to drop you when you were a baby. I suppose you must have been quite slippery."

"You couldn't be any prettier than you are now," Beth told Amy. "And I think your nose is extremely aristocratic. For an American, that is."

"Beth's right," said Jo. "A true patriot wouldn't care so much for an aristocratic nose, Amy. You are a true patriot, aren't you?"

"As much a one as you," Amy said. "But there's nothing in the Constitution that prevents me from wanting a truly beautiful nose."

"You're beautiful enough as you are," said Meg. "What else would you like?"

Amy thought about it. She knew she was pretty. Her shiny blond hair fell in lovely curls, and her eyes were as blue as cornflowers. Still, an aristocratic nose would help, but beyond sleeping with a clothespin on her nose there was little she could do to make it perfect.

"I'd like to be a real, professional artist," she said. "Someone who sells her paintings for lots and lots of money."

"I'd like that too," Jo said. "For you're a generous girl, Amy, and sure to share your wealth with your less fortunate sisters!"

The girls laughed. They were still laughing when their parents entered the parlor.

"What a wonderful greeting," Father said. "My little women enjoying themselves so."

"Father, Marmee!" the girls cried, and although they had seen their parents just a few hours earlier, they rushed into their arms and exchanged embraces.

"It is good to see you so happy," Marmee said. "Especially after the conversation we just had with the Emersons."

"Why, Marmee?" Beth asked. "Everything's all right with them, isn't it?"

"With them, yes," Father replied. "But not with the nation."

"You mean the Southern states seceding?" Jo asked. "President Lincoln will keep the country together. I'm sure of it."

"It will take more than words," said Father. "It was in the newspapers. The Confederates have fired upon Fort Sumter."

"Where's that, Father?" asked Meg. Amy was glad Meg had asked, as she didn't care to appear ignorant.

"It's in Charleston, South Carolina. The Union soldiers were asked to surrender but refused, and the Southerners fired upon them."

"How terrible," Meg said. "Were there fatalities?"

"Fortunately not," said Father. "But we'd be naive to think there won't be. War has begun, and with war there is always loss and suffering."

"I wish I were a boy," said Jo. "I'd enlist right away to fight for the Union and for the end of slavery."

"I'm glad I have daughters and no sons," said Marmee. "I know it's selfish of me, but at least I don't have to worry about any of you dying in battle. No matter how noble the cause."

"You aren't going to go off to be a soldier, are you, Father?" asked Beth.

"I'm too old, I'm afraid," Father said. "But there must be something I can do. All these years, I've fought for abolition. But what are words when young men are going to sacrifice their lives?"

"Words are what you have to offer," said Marmee. "And prayers too, for a quick resolution to this war."

War. Amy thrilled at the very word. She had no desire to be a boy and go off to fight. But, like Jo, she found the idea of war exciting. Handsome young men in uniform, fighting for a just and noble cause.

She supposed some of the men fighting for the South were handsome as well, but she didn't care. They were certain to lose and to realize how wrong they were about everything.

"It's a good war, isn't it, Father?" she asked.

Father sighed. "All wars are evil. But in this case, there's a greater evil, and that's slavery. So in some ways, it's a good war. But I pray it will be a short one, with as little bloodshed as possible."

"That's what we all should pray for," Marmee said.

Amy thought about her nose. It was selfish of her to wish for a nicer one when young men were going to risk their lives for the freedom of others.

"I'll pray for a short war, Father," Amy said. "And for freedom for the slaves."

Her father smiled at her. "I know you will, Amy. And I know my daughters will do everything they can to help the cause. Sacrifices will have to be made. There are always sacrifices in times of war. But you'll do what you have to to alleviate the suffering of others."

"We will, I promise," said Meg. "We'll do whatever we can for the Union and for abolition."

Amy wondered what she would have to sacrifice. Anything but the clothespin, she thought, then realized she was still being selfish. Anything at all, she promised. She would sacrifice anything at all for the Union and abolition.

# CHAPTER 2

"Did you hear, Amy?" her friend Katy Brown asked her in the school yard on Monday.

"About the war, you mean?" asked Amy. "Father told us all about it."

"No, not that. About the photographer."

"What photographer?" Amy asked.

"His name is Mr. Knox," Katy said. "And he's come to Concord to take pictures with his camera."

"It's so exciting," Mary Kingsley declared. "Mama says she's going to have her picture taken. She says it's all the rage in New York and Paris."

"My father had his picture taken already," Amy said. "Last year in New York. Mathew Brady took it right before he took Mr. Lincoln's."

"I think it must be the most wonderful thing in the world," said Katy. "I hope Mama says Mr. Knox can take my picture, but I'm sure his photographs are fearfully expensive."

"The picture of Father certainly looks like him," Amy said. "But he always says he prefers my sketches of him."

"You're a wonderful artist," Mary said. "But I'd still love to have my photograph taken. Wouldn't you?"

"I suppose," Amy said. The girls walked into the school together, and Amy forced herself to concentrate on her schoolwork. It wasn't easy to work on sums when there were war and photography to think about.

After school Amy decided to walk into town before heading home. None of her sisters was there to object. Beth's acute shyness had required that their father school her at home. And as for Meg and Jo, they went to a completely different school. So there was no one to make Amy go straight home. And this day, Amy felt in no hurry to get back.

Concord was a bustling town. Amy knew just about all the people who lived and worked there, and as she walked its streets, she said hello to the grocer, the druggist, and the constable.

It was in front of the stationer's that Amy saw the sign. DAVID KNOX, PHOTOGRAPHER. ONE FLIGHT UP.

Amy looked up. The second story had a large window. Amy supposed if she crossed the street, she might be able to see into the window. She was debating whether she should do this when a young man walked out through the door next to the stationer's shop.

"What do you think of my sign?" the young man asked.

11

"Oh," said Amy. "Are you the photographer?"

"That I am. David Knox at your service. A better photographer than sign painter, I might add."

"I think the sign is fine," said Amy. "Has it brought you much business?"

"I only arrived on Friday," Mr. Knox said. "I'm optimistic that business will develop as more people learn I'm here."

"People already know," Amy said. "Katy Brown and Mary Kingsley couldn't stop talking about you today."

"Are they likely to have their pictures taken?" Mr. Knox asked.

"If their mothers let them." Amy smiled. "They're my age."

"Let's hope for generous mothers, then," said Mr. Knox. "Do you think your mother is likely to let me take *your* picture?"

"I'm sure she'd like to," Amy said. "My father had his picture taken by Mathew Brady in New York City."

13

"Did he really? Mathew Brady is my idol. I hope someday to work with him. But meantime, I'm in Concord, hoping Mary Brown's and Katy Kingsley's mothers will prove generous."

"*Katy* Brown," Amy corrected. "*Mary* Kingsley."

"Right," Mr. Knox said. "I won't mix them up again."

"How much does it cost to have one's picture taken?" Amy asked.

"I charge five dollars. Considerably less than Mathew Brady, I'll wager."

"Five dollars," Amy said. "That's still a lot of money."

"But you get a beautiful photograph to cherish forever," Mr. Knox replied. "Taken by the next Mathew Brady. A work of art, if I do say so myself."

"I'm an artist, too," Amy said. "I draw."

"I knew it. I knew I was speaking to a fellow artist," Mr. Knox said. "Would you care to come upstairs and examine my work?"

14

"I'd love to," Amy said. She followed Mr. Knox up to his studio.

Beth had described to Amy Mathew Brady's gallery, which Beth had seen during a visit to New York City with their parents. It had been sumptuous, with velvet drapes and golden wallpaper and photographs of all the great and important people of the time. She had been especially impressed by a photograph of the Prince of Wales. Mr. Knox's studio was not remotely similar. A few photographs hung from the walls, but none of anyone Amy recognized. She did, however, appreciate the large window and the skylight, which made the room quite bright. There were also many mirrors to reflect the sunlight.

"Light is everything," Mr. Knox said. "But you must know that."

Amy nodded. "What's that?" she asked, pointing at a strange-looking device.

"It's a head clamp," he replied. "It takes a long time to take a photograph, and if the subject should happen to move at just the wrong moment, the whole picture is ruined. That's a supporting stand, for the subject to recline against. And these are my backdrops. I like to provide a choice. See? This one is an outdoor view. And this one is an elegant parlor. And this is just a black backdrop, for people who prefer a more classic setting."

"And this is the camera," Amy said, walking over to a strange, boxlike structure. She had never seen a camera before and had often wondered what one looked like.

"That it is," Mr. Knox said.

The camera was placed on top of a three-legged stand. Sticking out of the box was the lens.

"And it really takes pictures?" Amy asked as she looked through the lens.

"I like to think *I* take the pictures," Mr. Knox said. "But yes, that's the camera that I use for my portraits."

Amy looked at the pictures next. The people standing in front of the outdoor scene, the parlor, and the plain black backdrop all looked prosperous and somber.

"None of them are smiling," she said.

"It's hard to smile after you've been posing for so long," Mr. Knox replied. "And the mirrors reflect light into your eyes. Someday I suppose cameras will work faster, and then people won't look quite so serious. It's only been twenty-five years since cameras were invented, and it's remarkable how much they've improved in just that time. Did you know there were photographs taken of the Crimean War? Can you imagine if there were pictures of the Revolution or the War of 1812?"

"Do you think there will be pictures taken of the war now?" Amy asked.

Mr. Knox looked serious. "I'm sure there will be. And of all other wars that are fought. And through those pictures people will see just what war really is, the pain and the devastation. The world will never view war in the same way again." He turned to Amy and

smiled. "But in the meantime, I'll take portraits of the well-to-do in New England," he
said. "Five dollars for a picture that your family can cherish forever."

Five dollars, Amy thought. For five dollars,
she could have her very own photograph.

Amy knew what she wanted. Now it was
just a question of figuring out how to get it.

# CHAPTER 3

Amy's only wealthy relative was Aunt March. She was Father's aunt by marriage and had been widowed since Amy was four. Amy remembered Uncle March only a little, though everyone said he had been a very nice man. Nobody described Aunt March as very nice.

Still, she was a relative and she had money, and Amy didn't know where else to turn. Not that she intended to beg for anything. The Marches had too much pride to ask Aunt March to help them. But maybe Amy would find Aunt March in a generous mood. The only way to know was to pay her a visit.

There were crocuses blooming in Aunt March's garden, and daffodils were sticking their heads out of the ground. Amy loved the springtime and the opportunity it gave her to draw flowers. Just seeing the crocuses made her confident Aunt March would help her out.

She knocked on the door, and Aunt March's butler opened it. "Hello, Williams," Amy said. "Is my aunt receiving?" She loved how grown-up she sounded.

"I will inform her of your presence," Williams declared, sounding very grand. Amy loved visiting people who had butlers. Everyone she knew had a housekeeper, and most of her friends had maidservants as well, but butlers were a special treat.

"You may come in," Williams said when he had returned to the hallway. "Mrs. March will see you."

"Thank you," Amy said. She followed Williams to the front parlor and found Aunt March sitting at her desk, where she had been tending to her correspondence.

Amy walked over to her great-aunt and gave her a kiss.

"To what do I owe the pleasure of this visit?" Aunt March asked. "You never come to see me, Amy, unless there's a reason."

"That's not true," Amy said, although she knew it was. "I love visiting with you, Aunt March. I would do it more often, except school keeps me so busy."

"And what are you learning in school these days?"

Amy tried to remember. Aunt March had a remarkable ability to knock all sensible thoughts out of her head. "The usual things," she finally said. "Spelling. Arithmetic. Geography." She was sure there were other things as well, but she couldn't recall what they might be.

"I was a fine speller in my day," Aunt March declared. "And I always had a gift for figures. Knowledge comes in handy no matter what your station in life. I'm glad to see you're getting a good education, Amy. Pretty blond curls will get you only so far. It's what you know that can raise you out of poverty."

Amy wasn't so sure she was in poverty, but then again, if she had had money, she wouldn't have been visiting her aunt. And since she wanted something, it made sense to be agreeable. "You're right, Aunt March," she said. "And I'll work hard at my schooling. I'd like to be a good speller, the way you are."

"Spell 'necessary,'" said Aunt March.

"I beg your pardon?"

"The word 'necessary.' Spell it," repeated Aunt March. "I know I could spell 'necessary' when I was your age."

Amy wasn't a very good speller, and it was particularly nerve-racking to have to spell such a hard word without any time to think

about it. "N-E-C-E-S-S-E-R-Y," she said.
" 'Necessary.' "

Aunt March humphed. Amy didn't think that was a good sign.

"Did I put too many esses in it?" Amy asked. She frequently did.

"It's 'A-R-Y,' " Aunt March said. "Not 'E-R-Y.' Perhaps that school of yours isn't doing such a fine job after all."

"Perhaps not," Amy said. "But it's the best we can afford. Even with Beth learning at home, Father and Marmee have to pay for Meg's and Jo's education as well as mine. I'm sure they know how to spell 'necessary.' I think it's a word you learn when you're twelve."

"It's a necessary word to know," said Aunt March. "Haw. Haw. A little joke there, my girl. Necessary word."

"Oh, yes," Amy said, and laughed dutifully. She wished, not for the first time, that she had been born rich and allowed to stay that way.

"You were right, Aunt March," she said. "I did come here for a reason."

"And not just to spell words with your lonely old aunt?" Aunt March said. "What a surprise."

"Of course I enjoy spelling words with you," Amy said. "But I really came to ask you if you had heard about the photographer."

"What photographer?"

"His name is Mr. Knox, and he's just opened a studio in town," said Amy. "Above the stationer's. I've seen his work. He takes beautiful portraits."

"And you think I should have one taken," said Aunt March. "Whatever for?"

Since that hadn't been what Amy had been thinking, it took her a moment to come up with a reply. "I know Father and Marmee would treasure one," she said. "Marmee loves the picture of Father so. It's 1861, Aunt March. All the truly fashionable people have their pictures taken: President

Lincoln, Queen Victoria—everybody worth knowing."

"Perhaps you're right," said Aunt March. "You say his studio is above the stationer's?"

"It is," Amy said. "And his work is of the highest quality. Almost as good as Mathew Brady's."

"That Brady person took your father's picture," Aunt March said. "It is peculiar that your father, poor as a church mouse, should have his photograph on display, while a lady of my position has never had hers taken."

"Very peculiar," Amy agreed. "If I were you, Aunt March, I'd go there tomorrow and have my picture taken. You even have a choice of backdrops. There's pastoral and parlor and classic."

"Very well," said Aunt March. "You've convinced me it's the necessary thing to do. Thank you, Amy. You may go now."

Amy gave her great-aunt a farewell kiss,

then left the parlor. She wasn't sure how Aunt March had managed it, but somehow she'd gotten what Amy had wanted for herself, and Amy had gotten nothing in return.

Nothing except a spelling lesson, that is. Amy shook her head. Somehow she was going to have to convince someone of how necessary it was to give her five dollars.

# CHAPTER 4

*T*hat evening, when everyone was talking about the war, Amy went upstairs to her bedroom and took her hidden box of money from behind her books. It was a very small box, one Marmee had given her years before when Father had presented Marmee with a cameo for her birthday. Amy had loved the little box, almost as much as Marmee had loved the cameo, and Marmee had given it to her to hold her own treasures.

Amy didn't have a lot of treasures. She didn't have a lot of money either, so she kept what she had in the little box. There was no reason to hide it, since no one in the family would have dreamed of stealing, but Amy liked the idea of something of hers being private and secret. There wasn't much room for privacy in their house, and none of them was very good with secrets.

Amy emptied the box onto her bed and counted her life savings. There were two dollars and twenty-six cents.

Since Amy loved to spend money, she was a little surprised she had that much saved. Then she remembered she was planning to buy her first set of oils with the money.

All great painters painted in oils, and Amy was determined to be a great painter. And one didn't simply purchase oil paints. One had to get canvases and brushes as well, and a smock to wear over one's dress. It was an expensive proposition to be a great painter. Amy knew it would cost a great deal more than two dollars and twenty-six cents.

his study, a handsome
knew how much Fa-
joy reading all those
ed if she might some-
to allow them to bor-
articular moment, she

arch," she said, trying
professional. "I'm an
oor."

Laurence said. "That
n. Have you much ex-

rowned heads of Eu-
t is to say, I've made
gs. And of Mr. Lin-
I draw from life as

Ir. Laurence. "I hear

re is a photographer
Mr. Knox. His work
k a hand-drawn por-

2

And that was less than half of what she
would need for her photograph to be taken.
Amy imagined Katy and Mary and Aunt
March having their pictures taken, and it
seemed terribly unfair that she was less than
halfway to having enough money and thus
would be deprived of owning such a wonderful thing.

Amy also reasoned that though everyone
told her she drew excellent portraits, she had
no gift for self-portraiture. Her nose dis-
pleased her too much. And if she was to be a
great painter, surely people would want to
know what she had looked like as a girl. She
knew she would have been thrilled to see
what Raphael and Rembrandt had looked like
as boys.

When Amy set her mind to something, she
could usually come up with a solution. That
night she pondered how to raise two dollars
and seventy-four cents, and by the morning
she had a plan.

She went to school that day and listened as Katy and Mary chattered about whether their mothers would be going to the photographer. "Of course they should have their pictures taken," Amy said. "My aunt March is going. It's quite the thing. And Mr. Knox's work is of the highest caliber. Why, he's almost as good as Mathew Brady."

"I'll tell Mama that," said Katy. "She knows what a fine lady Mrs. March is."

"Just like Queen Victoria," Amy agreed. "Only better, because she's an American."

When the school day ended, Amy ran home. She dashed past Beth, who, having been home all day, always welcomed the return of her sisters, and raced to their bedroom, where she got her drawing pad and her pencils. Amy knew only one other wealthy person in Concord. Not that she really knew him. But he was her neighbor, and that meant she just about knew him. Or so she had decided.

Mr. Laurence was in book-lined room. Am ther and Jo would e books, and she wond day ask Mr. Laurenc row some. But at this had other plans.

"My name is Amy to sound grown-up a artist and I live next

"I can see that," M you are an artist, I m perience?"

"I have drawn the rope," said Amy. "T copies of their pain coln's. And of cour well."

"Of course," said you want to draw m

Amy nodded. "T in town," she said. is excellent, but I t

trait is so much more significant. Don't you?"

"Oh, yes," said Mr. Laurence. "Far more significant."

"I'd paint you in oils, but I don't have any," said Amy. "They cost more than I can afford at this stage in my career. But I can do a lovely pencil sketch of you, and it will cost far less than a painting, or even a photograph."

"And how much would that be?" Mr. Laurence asked.

"A photograph costs five dollars," said Amy. "I will sketch you for two dollars and seventy-four cents. That's a little more than half of the cost of the photograph."

"It is indeed," said Mr. Laurence. "And what do you propose I do with this sketch once it's completed?"

"You could frame it," Amy said. "Or you could send it to someone you love. But I'd keep it. I intend to be famous someday, and then the picture would have great value. Far

33

more than the two dollars and seventy-four cents I'm charging."

"It sounds like quite a bargain," Mr. Laurence said. "Very well, young lady. I have work to do. Why don't you sketch me as I read through my correspondence?"

"Really?" Amy said. "I mean, certainly. Sit there, if you would. By the light."

Mr. Laurence followed Amy's instructions. The late-afternoon light shone through the window. Amy pulled up a chair and positioned herself so that she could sketch Mr. Laurence at a three-quarter angle. She drew faces better in three-quarter than in full or half.

"So you say a photographer has come to town," Mr. Laurence remarked as Amy began to sketch.

"His name is Mr. Knox," Amy said. "He's almost as good as Mathew Brady. I know because my father had his picture taken by Mathew Brady. But Father says he prefers the sketch of him I made."

"Still, I might go to this photographer," said Mr. Laurence. "If only to compare his work to yours."

"I think that's a fine idea," said Amy. "Now, if you would please keep quiet. I have trouble with mouths when they're moving."

"Naturally," Mr. Laurence said. He became engrossed in his correspondence and hardly paid attention to Amy as she continued to sketch away.

"I've finished," Amy said a while later, trying to keep from sounding too prideful. Truly, her portrait of Mr. Laurence was the best she'd ever drawn.

"Why, that's quite good," Mr. Laurence said, examining it carefully. "You are an artist, Miss March."

"Yes, sir," Amy said. "Do you think it's worth two dollars and seventy-four cents?"

"At the very least," Mr. Laurence said. He put his hand into his pocket and took out some money. "Here," he said, counting the

change carefully. "Two dollars and seventy-five cents. Keep the penny."

"Thank you, sir," said Amy. She now had five dollars and one cent. Five dollars for her photograph to be taken, and one cent to go toward her oils.

# CHAPTER 5

*A*my went home that evening in the most joyful of moods. She had set a goal for herself and had accomplished it. Even more satisfying, she'd received no charity from Aunt March and had earned her first real money as an artist. Truly, the world was a splendid place.

So Amy was surprised when no one at home seemed half as happy as she. It was a lovely April day, and that alone should have made them all cheerful.

"It's Marmee," Beth said to Amy when Amy asked what was the matter. "She's been in tears all afternoon. But she won't tell us why."

Amy suddenly felt very frightened. She had seen Marmee cry, but not very often and never without good cause. Something awful must have happened, and Amy dreaded hearing what it was.

After grace at suppertime that evening, Father looked at his wife and daughters. "I have something I must tell you," he said. "Your mother and I have discussed it most of the day, and the time has come for you to be informed."

The March girls, usually full of good cheer and conversation, were all silent and solemn.

"President Lincoln has called for seventy-five thousand volunteers," Father said. "These volunteers will fight for the preservation of the Union, and, I hope, for an end to slavery."

"Are you volunteering, Father?" asked Jo.

"But you can't," said Meg. "You said you were too old."

"I am too old to be a soldier," said Father.

"But armies have other needs. Young men in battle have spiritual requirements far greater than any I can tend to in Concord. I am going to volunteer my services as a chaplain."

"Bully for you!" cried Jo. "Helping our soldiers in such a fine way."

"But, Father," Meg said, "won't there be danger?"

"I suspect so," Father replied. "In wartime there always is. But I'm sure the Lord will watch over me as I know He will watch over those I love."

Amy knew now why Marmee had been crying. She felt like crying herself.

"What will become of us?" Beth asked. "Can we go to the battlefield with you, Father?"

Father laughed. "I think not, Bethy," he said. "Although I'm sure you would make a fine Florence Nightingale. And you, Jo, were born to be Molly Pitcher. No, you can best serve the needs of our family and of our country by staying home and helping each other."

"I know one way I can help," said Meg. "Marmee, Father, the time has come for me to leave school and get employment."

"No," said Marmee. "There's no need."

"Yes, there is," Meg said, and Amy thought she'd never seen Meg so grown up. "I've learned as much in school as I really want to, Marmee. And you know how much I love little children. I've been thinking for months now about getting employment as a nursery governess. I'll stay on in school until the end of the year and then see what sort of work I can get."

"If that's your desire, you have my blessing," said Father.

"I want to leave school too," said Jo. "Oh, not to be a soldier, although if I could, I surely would. No, to do something far more dangerous."

"Whatever are you talking about?" asked Marmee.

"I should like to work as Aunt March's companion," said Jo. "Now, there's some-

41

thing that could put fear in the hearts of all those Southern gentlemen."

"Aunt March's companion?" Father asked. "Has she spoken to you about it?"

"Yes, she has," said Jo. "We discussed the possibility of my working as her companion this summer and, if we find it suits us, of my staying on in that capacity. She finds me entertaining, and while I can't really say the same about her, she has a good library and a good heart. Besides, school is boring, and all I need to know to be a writer I've learned already—spelling and grammar and whatnot. The rest will come from experience. If I work for Aunt March, I can continue to live at home, which I would truly prefer. Give me your blessing, Father."

"That you have, my child," Father said. "You and Meg both. You are both fine, unselfish girls, and I'm proud of you."

"I'll stay home and help Marmee and Hannah," said Beth. "There will be more to do with Meg and Jo both working."

"And I . . . ," said Amy, but she stopped, since she had no idea what kind of sacrifice she could make. She was too young to go to work, and she really didn't think Marmee and Hannah needed another pair of hands. "I'll be good, Father, and never cause any trouble."

"You never do, my child," said Father. "None of my girls does. You are brave soldiers and the greatest joy a man could know."

"We'll pray for you each day, Father," Meg said. "And for the soldiers you'll be consoling."

"And we'll knit slippers for them as well," said Jo. "And sew sheets and do whatever else we can for the cause."

"And I'll work on my nursing skills," said Beth. "In case they're needed. Although I'm sure the war will last just a few more weeks, and the South will come to its senses and realize what an evil slavery is."

"I pray that you're right," Father said. "But

we must be prepared for a long and arduous battle."

"We will be, Father," Jo promised.

Amy looked at her parents and her sisters. She knew her world would never be the same. She only wished there were something more she could do to help with the long fight to come.

# CHAPTER 6

Amy found Meg in the bedroom Meg shared with Jo. Amy was pleased to find her oldest sister alone, and she sat down on Jo's bed. "You and Jo will really be leaving school?" she asked.

"So it would seem," Meg replied. "It's funny. I didn't know Jo's plans and she didn't know mine, but we both had the same idea. Even if Father weren't going off to war, this family could use a bit more income."

"I wish there were something I could do," Amy said. "Would it help if I left school?"

"Not in the slightest," Meg replied. "You

45

like school and you do well with your studies. Besides, there's still a great deal you have to learn. Spelling and grammar and whatnot, as Jo so elegantly phrased it."

"But I could find work," Amy said. "Children my age work all over America. As servants, or in factories." She was afraid Meg might agree that this was a good idea, but still she felt she had to suggest it.

"You know how Father and Marmee feel about child labor." Meg shook her head. "They would never permit it. It would upset them to know you were even thinking of such a thing. Promise me you won't say anything like that to them, Amy. With Father going away so shortly, they don't need to have you bringing up such a scheme."

Amy was more than happy to make that promise. "I won't say a thing about it," she said. "But I still wish there were something I could do."

"You can be a well-behaved little girl," Meg said. "You can work hard at your studies and your art. You can get into fewer fights with Jo, even though she does provoke you. You can assist Marmee and Hannah with their work. And you can worry less about your nose and more about your soul. How's that for a list of things you can do?"

Amy thought it was quite the dreariest list she'd ever heard. "I suppose I'm too young to be a nurse," she said.

"Just a bit," said Meg. "And I'm sure the war will be over in a matter of months. Perhaps even before your eleventh birthday. What a present that would be for us all, to have Father back home so soon."

"Maybe the war will end right away," Amy said, "before Father ever has the chance to go."

"That would be wonderful," Meg replied. "But I don't think we should count on it."

"No, I suppose not," Amy said, and she left Meg's room. It was impossible for her to imagine life without Father. The year before, he, Marmee, and Beth had spent a week together in New York City, and it had felt like forever to Amy. Back home, she and Jo had quarreled daily. Of course now, with Jo working, Amy supposed she'd see less of her as well. And Marmee and Beth would remain home. But not to see Father every evening at the dinner table . . . not to hear his baritone harmonizing with all their sopranos . . . not to feel the warm comfort of his embraces or to smell his pipe tobacco or to listen to and learn from his Sunday sermons—Amy wondered how she would endure.

She went downstairs in search of someone to comfort her and found her mother in the parlor looking at the photograph of Father.

"Amy," Marmee said, "stand with me and admire how Mr. Brady captured your father's spirit in this picture."

"I'm so glad we have the photograph," Amy said. "Father looks so handsome in it."

"Yes, he does." Marmee lovingly traced her husband's image with her fingers. "I'm sure he'll be the handsomest chaplain in the Union

Army." She gave Amy a hug. "I knew it would be a good idea to have this photograph taken," she added. "And now I know why I was right. It will keep me company during the long days that Father must spend away from us."

Father walked into the parlor. "Admiring my portrait again?" he asked.

"All the more for knowing it will stay with us when you are gone," said Marmee.

"I wish Mr. Brady had taken one of you as well," said Father. "You will be constantly in my heart, but with a photograph of you by my side, I think I would feel even closer to you."

"The memory of me will just have to do," said Marmee. "Perhaps we can ask Amy to sketch me for you. I know how you love her drawings."

"No," said Amy. "I mean, I have a much better idea."

"And what is that?" Father asked.

"There's a photographer in town," said

Amy. "Mr. Knox. He can take Marmee's picture. I'm sure he'd do a splendid job."

"What do you say, dear?" asked Father. "I know what a comfort such a picture would be for me."

"How much does it cost?" asked Marmee.

"Five dollars," Amy replied.

Marmee shook her head and smiled. "We don't have that sort of money."

"I do," Amy said. "I have five dollars and one cent, and I've been saving it to have my picture taken. But I'd so much rather he take your picture, Marmee, so that Father might have it. Please say yes."

"Five dollars," Marmee said. "That would pay for a lot of milk and eggs."

"But I don't want to spend it on milk and eggs," said Amy. "And it's my money. You simply have to say yes, Marmee. Please. Everyone else is doing something to help, and I'm too young to do anything really wonderful. But I can do this. Mr. Knox can take your picture, and then Father can carry it with him. Oh, Marmee, please say yes."

Father nodded. "It would mean so much to me," he said. "I would have a picture of you to cherish, and it would be all the sweeter because my youngest gave it to me."

Still Marmee hesitated.

"Eggs and milk won't last forever," Amy said. "But this photograph will. And you always say we shouldn't throw our money away on things that won't last."

Marmee and Father laughed. "All right," said Mother. "You've convinced me. I'll go to the photographer tomorrow."

Amy hugged her mother. She knew that the sacrifice she was making was a small one compared to those the other members of her family were offering to the Union cause. But it was all she had, and the little bit of pain she felt at the loss of a photograph of herself made the gift even finer.

# CHAPTER 7

*A*my wanted Mr. Knox to know just whose mother Marmee was, and she insisted that Marmee wait until the school day had ended before going into town to have her picture taken. When Amy's sisters learned of the plan, they insisted on accompanying Marmee as well.

The studio was bustling. Amy was surprised at how many people were there to meet Mr. Knox. Where just a few days before the place had been empty, now there were at least a half dozen people waiting to have their pictures taken.

Marmee sat down on one of the benches while the girls examined Mr. Knox's work. Amy held on to her five dollars. She glared at the other customers, willing them to be done so that Marmee's picture could be taken. After all, how many of them had fathers or husbands going off to war? Marmee was the important one, and it was unfair that she should have to wait.

But wait she did, and as they all waited, the sky outside grew darker and darker. "I think it might rain," Jo said.

"It can't," said Amy. "Mr. Knox needs light to take his pictures."

"There's nothing we can do about it," Marmee said. "If it rains, it rains. I'll simply have to come back some other time."

"But Father will be leaving soon," said Amy. "If only these other people would leave, Mr. Knox would be able to take your picture right away."

But of course nobody left. And by the time Mr. Knox had completed the last of their portraits, the sky was so dark, even Amy knew that no picture could be taken of Marmee that day.

Mr. Knox came out of his studio and walked over to Marmee and the girls where they sat in his gallery area. "Why, it's Amy March," he said. "I'm pleased to see you again."

"This is Mr. Knox, Marmee," Amy said. "Mr. Knox, this is my mother, Mrs. March, and my sisters, Meg and Jo and Beth."

"I'm pleased to meet you all," said Mr. Knox. "Miss Amy told me about Mr. Brady's portrait of Mr. March. I would be most interested in seeing it sometime, if it wouldn't be too much of an imposition."

"We'd be pleased to have you come by the house," Marmee said. "In fact, it was Mr. Brady's picture that convinced us I should have my photograph taken."

"Here," said Amy, handing over her five dollars. "Is there still enough light to take Marmee's picture?"

"I'm afraid not," said Mr. Knox.

"Oh, dear," Meg said. "We really wanted the picture taken as soon as possible. Father is going off to be a chaplain for the Union Army, and we want him to have Marmee's picture when he goes."

"I have an idea," said Mr. Knox. "Shall I come over to your house tomorrow morning with my camera? I can take the photograph of Mrs. March outdoors with natural light, and I can see the Mathew Brady picture at the same time."

"We wouldn't want to inconvenience you," Marmee said.

"It wouldn't be an inconvenience at all," Mr. Knox replied. "In fact, I've written to Mr. Brady to offer my service as a photographer for the Union. President Lincoln has told him he wants pictures taken at the battlefields, and I feel it would be my way of helping the cause. The more practice I can get with outdoor photography, the better."

"A portrait is hardly a battlefield," Marmee said.

"True," Mr. Knox said. "But sunlight is sunlight. You would be doing me a favor if you agreed."

Marmee smiled. "Then I suppose I must."

"Oh, yes," said Jo. "Father will much prefer a picture of you taken at home. He'll get two mementos for the price of one!"

"We're agreed, then?" Mr. Knox said. "Very well. I'll see you in the morning."

"Not unless I tell you where we live," Marmee pointed out, and with the help of her daughters and the use of pencil and paper, she made up a map that Mr. Knox would be able to follow the next day.

And follow it he did. He appeared at the Marches' home bright and early, leaving his horse tied to a gatepost. And it *was* a bright day, the previous evening's showers having washed all the clouds from the sky.

"I hope the weather is this fine for my future picture-taking," Mr. Knox said as he set up his camera. He had already spent a few minutes inside the March house, meeting Father, examining the Brady photograph, and enjoying a cup of coffee.

"So you plan to take pictures of the war?" Father asked as he watched Mr. Knox at work.

"Yes, sir, I do," Mr. Knox said. "If Mr. Brady will have me. I truly believe that pictures tell the truth, and the truth is the strongest weapon that right has on its side."

"I agree with you there," said Father. "And what did you think of Mr. Brady's picture of me?"

"I think it portrays a man of conviction and courage," Mr. Knox replied.

"You see, Father?" Jo said. "Photographs do tell the truth."

"In that case, a photograph of my wife will show a perfect angel," Father said.

"I'll do my best to convey that," Mr. Knox said. "Now, Mrs. March, if you would just stand here, by this willow tree. Lean against it if you wish, while I set up for the photograph."

"I feel as though I'm playacting," Marmee said. "My daughters love to act, but I've gotten accustomed to merely being the audience."

"Having your portrait taken *is* a bit of playacting," Mr. Knox agreed. "We all wish to seem our best, and none of us can be that at all times. Please stand perfectly still."

"But the sun is in my eyes," Marmee said.

"You can keep your eyes closed for a few seconds longer, then," he said. "But open them when I tell you to, and try your hardest to keep them open."

"How I wish Amy were drawing my portrait," Marmee said. "She never seems to care if my eyes are open or closed."

"Now, Marmee," Meg said. "Photography is all the rage. Isn't it, Mr. Knox?"

"It would seem to be in Concord," he said. "Open your eyes now, Mrs. March. Very good. Now let me take another picture, just to be sure we get a good one." He snapped a second time.

"So the people of Concord have been keeping you busy?" Father asked.

"They have indeed," Mr. Knox said. "And it's all because of Miss Amy here."

"Me?" said Amy. "What have I done now?"

Everybody laughed.

"Miss Amy has been telling some very important people what a good photographer I am," Mr. Knox said. "Your aunt, Mrs. March, for one, and Mr. Laurence, for another. And when people heard that Mrs. March and Mr. Laurence had come in to have their pictures taken, they followed suit. My business has been booming."

"What a shame you have to leave it when it's become so successful," Meg said.

"I would have anyway," Mr. Knox said. "There are a limited number of people in the area, and once I finished with their portraits, I would have to move on. But thanks to Miss

wing Wednesday, Amy awoke
sense of dread. The day had
hen Father would be joining
ps.
ver to Beth's bed and saw that
already awake. "Today's the
l. "We must be very brave for
rmee."
my said, although she wasn't
at all. She got out of bed,
l, and walked downstairs. Fa-
ee were already up, and Amy
's and Jo's voices upstairs.

64

Amy, I've earned quite a bit of money in a
very short time, and I'll be able to send what
I've earned to my parents to help them out
when I'm working with Mr. Brady."

"Just think, Amy," Jo said. "That mouth of
yours has finally done some good."

"Jo!" Meg reprimanded her. "Amy, I didn't
know you knew Mr. Laurence."

"I drew his picture to earn the money for
Marmee's," Amy said.

"That was enterprising of you," Jo said.

"Indeed," Father said. "And I'm delighted
you did, Amy, for your mother's picture will
bring me great comfort in the months to
come."

"And how would you feel, sir, about a photograph of your daughters as well?" Mr.
Knox asked.

"We can't afford it," Amy said. "I've already given you my only five dollars."

"But I owe you something for all the business you've sent my way," Mr. Knox said.
"And my camera is here already, so I might as

61

well make
could carr
March?"

"I know
would be
gift."

"It's no
commissio
be honore

"Oh, w
speak for
too, Jo. A
light to b
picture ta

C

The follo
with a
come v
the Union tro
She looked
her sister was
day," Beth sai
Father and M
"I know," A
feeling brave
washed, dresse
ther and Marr
could hear Me

"The pictures of you are so beautiful," Father was saying as Amy joined them in the parlor. "Mr. Knox did a splendid job."

"Am I really that pretty?" Marmee asked. "I know the girls are, but I somehow can't recognize myself in that picture."

"You heard what Mr. Knox said," replied Father. "Photographs tell the truth."

"You are that pretty, Marmee," Amy said, looking at her mother's picture for the hundredth time since Mr. Knox had brought it over two days earlier. "But it has a lot to do with the way the sunlight catches your eyes."

"You are an artist," Marmee said. "I wouldn't have known that if you hadn't pointed it out to me."

"I love you in sunlight," Father said. "I'll look at this picture and remember how you looked when we were wed. The sunlight caught your eyes that day as well." He lifted Marmee's hand and pressed it to his lips.

"I must say," Jo declared as she, Meg, and Beth entered the parlor, "that picture Mr.

Knox took of us is perfectly grand. Meg looks like the perfect lady she is, and Beth the perfect angel. Amy never looked prettier, and even I look almost presentable."

"More than that," Father said. "And this picture captures more than just your appearances, my girls."

"What does it say about us, Father?" Beth asked.

Father looked first at the picture, then at his daughters. "It shows your courage," he said. "Your willingness to try new things. It shows your lack of vanity, for you agreed to have the picture taken without having any time to fuss and primp."

Amy blushed. The truth was, she would have been delighted to have done just that, but she had been so thrilled to have her picture taken after all that she hadn't thought to object.

"Do you see all that in this picture, Father?" Beth asked.

"All that and more," replied Father. "I see four sisters whose love for each other is evi-

66

dent in the way they stand so close together. And whose love for their parents shines in their eyes, for it was us you were facing, and not just the camera."

"We do love you, Father," Meg said. "You and Marmee. You're the best parents we could ever wish for."

"And you are the best children a man could have," Father said. "Some men have said how sorry they are for me that I have four daughters and no sons, and I've thought what fools they are. It doesn't matter if your child is a son or a daughter. What matters is what sort of person that child is, and you, my daughters, are all a father could wish for."

"We're not perfect," Meg said.

"Far from it, I'm afraid," Jo agreed.

"I wouldn't know what to do with perfect children," Father said. "Even if they existed, I think they'd be far too dull for my tastes. No, I love my little women as they are, each of them with her own dreams and her own plans to achieve them."

"We'll miss you so, Father," Beth said.

"And I'll miss you," he replied. "But in many ways, I'll be taking you with me. I'll never be too lonely, for your love will accompany me. I'll never be too frightened, for your courage will give me strength. And I'll never be too downhearted, for your faith will be as one with mine."

There was a knock on the door.

"That must be Mr. Emerson," Father said. He took the photographs of his wife and daughters and put them in his valise.

"You will remember to write to me from Boston?" Marmee asked.

"And from wherever they send me after that," Father said. He walked outside, followed by his wife and daughters. "Good-bye, my children," he said. "Obey your mother in all things. And trust in the Lord to bring freedom to the oppressed and peace to this great land of ours."

"Good-bye, Father," the girls said, as one .

by one they exchanged farewell embraces with him.

Father stood still for a moment, looking at them. "I'll remember you always this way," he said. "With the sunlight catching your eyes." Then, exchanging a final kiss with his wife, Father left his home and began his journey to war.

"I know what I want most now, Jo," Amy said, trying not to cry. "I want Father to come home safely and soon."

"I know, Amy," Jo said, giving her youngest sister a comforting embrace. "That's what we all want. With all our hearts, that's what we all want most."

Pour in butter and mix well.
2. Gradually add milk and mix.
3. Stir in raisins.
4. Knead lightly and roll out on a lightly floured surface to 3/4-inch thickness.
5. Cut into rounds with a floured 1-1/2-inch cutter.
6. Place on lightly greased cookie sheet.
7. Brush tops of scones with milk.
8. Bake in preheated oven 10 to 15 minutes.
9. Remove from oven and allow to cool.

Makes about 12 scones.
Serve with butter or jam.

# RAISIN SCONES

*These rich biscuits are perfect for breakfast, a snack,
or four o'clock tea.*

INGREDIENTS

3 cups flour
1 teaspoon salt
1/2 teaspoon baking soda
2 ounces melted and cooled butter
1 cup milk (optional: make milk sour by
   adding 1/2 teaspoon lemon juice); plus
   more milk for brushing scones
1/2 cup dark raisins

Preheat oven to 450 degrees.
1. Sift flour, salt, and baking soda into a bowl.

# PORTRAITS OF LITTLE WOMEN ACTIVITIES

*Everyone loves a pretty box to keep treasures in.
Whether filled with jewelry, letters, or special mementos,
a box also adds a decorative touch to a bedroom.*

MATERIALS

Wrapping paper (the thicker the better) or
  shelf liner

Shoe box or gift box or any box with a lid

Scissors

Glue

Small paintbrush, foam or bristle (to spread
  glue)

Ruler

Pencil

Felt

Ribbon or piping

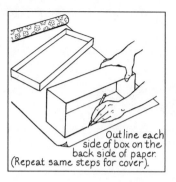

1. Lay box you are going to cover on its side on nonprinted side of paper.

2. Trace around box. Then, with a ruler, mark 1/2-inch point beyond box on each side. Cut paper at outer markings.

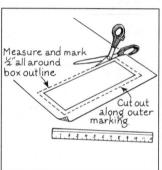

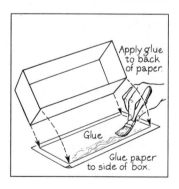

3. Glue paper onto box. *Note:* Make sure printed pattern goes in same direction on all sides of box.

4. Cut corners of excess paper up to box, then fold over and glue.

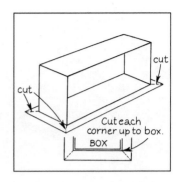

cut

cut

Cut each corner up to box.

BOX

GLUE

Apply glue to ½" edges including corners. Fold edges over, press in place.

5. Repeat steps 2 through 5 for other sides and lid.

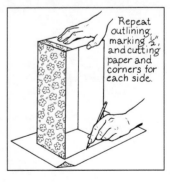

Repeat outlining, marking ½", and cutting paper and corners for each side.

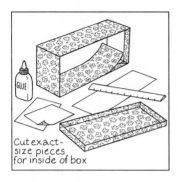

Cut exact-
size pieces
for inside of box

6. To cover inside of box, cut paper to actual size and glue on.

Place a fitted piece of unglued felt on the inside bottom of box.

7. Cut felt to line bottom of box (no need to glue).

Decorate with ribbon, piping, rick rack, etc.

8. To decorate, glue on ribbon or piping around sides or on lid.

It's the perfect box to hold your treasures. Makes a beautiful gift, too!

Read all about Louisa May Alcott's
unforgettable heroines in
Portraits of Little Women:

*Meg's Story*

*Jo's Story*

*Beth's Story*

*Amy's Story*

Here are sample chapters from each of the
other three delightful stories.

# Meg's Story

## CHAPTER 1

*M*eg March looked at her slate and sighed. Would the school day never end?

Ordinarily Meg enjoyed school. She loved to read, and she liked history as well. Her family was a part of American history. Two of her great-grandfathers had fought in the American Revolution. Even arithmetic, which was what her class was supposed to be working on just then, could be interesting.

But not on the first day of June. Not when the sun was shining and the classroom, which had been cold all winter long, was warm enough to encourage dozing. Not when she and her sisters were halfway through their most recent play, which would, of course, star Meg and Jo. Beth had agreed to play the piano for the play, and Amy was now old enough to memorize lines and could be given small parts to perform. It was certain to be their best production ever.

And the day was so lovely that when they got home, they could work on the play in the garden. So why wouldn't the school day end?

Meg looked quickly toward Jo's seat. Jo was a year younger, and they were in the same classroom. Beth and Amy were in a classroom for younger children. Meg wondered if they were as impatient as she was for lessons to be over. Jo was, she knew, but Jo was impatient about everything.

Meg feared she might explode, but fortunately the bell rang and the teacher dismissed the class. Meg noticed that he too seemed relieved, and she supposed it couldn't be fun to rein in the spirits of twenty-five children aged nine through eleven on a beautiful afternoon in June. Her parents frequently told her to be considerate of the feelings of others. Meg was pleased with herself that she cared about her teacher's feelings. She doubted Jo thought of him at all.

In fact, Jo had already escaped from the school by the time Meg reached the front door. Meg waited a moment, until Beth and Amy appeared, and then they walked out together. Jo, she noted, was racing with some of the boys from their class. Jo was the best runner in their class, and she never minded letting the boys know that.

"Jo isn't very ladylike," Amy said as they watched their sister win yet another race.

"Jo isn't ladylike at all," replied Meg.

"But you're a lady, Meg," said Beth.

"I'm more of one than Jo, but not nearly as much of one as Amy," Meg replied with a laugh.

"You can laugh," Amy said, "but I intend to marry great wealth someday, and I'll be more of a lady than anybody else in this town has ever been."

"Concord has many ladies," Beth said. "Doesn't it, Meg? Aunt March is a lady. And Marmee is the best lady of all."

"Amy means the kind of lady who wears silks and laces all the time," Meg said. "And doesn't make do with mended calicoes."

"You have no right to complain," said Amy. "I have it worst of all. Practically every dress I've ever owned you wore once, then Jo and then Beth. It wouldn't be so bad if it were just you, or even you and Beth. But Jo rips everything, and I spend half my life in patches." She looked so mournful that Meg burst out laughing again.

"Meg March! Wait for me!"

Meg turned around and saw Mary Howe calling for her. Mary was in the same class as Meg and Jo. And she was definitely Amy's idea of a lady. It was clear that Mary had never worn a patched piece of clothing in her life.

"Meg, I want to speak to you," Mary said as she joined the March sisters.

"Certainly, Mary," said Meg. Beth, always shy, was hiding as best she could behind Meg. Amy was staring straight at Mary, drinking in the details of Mary's perfect blue dress and its white lace collar.

"I'm having a picnic on Saturday," Mary announced. "My brother, Willie, and I. Mama said I could invite three girls and Willie could invite three boys. Willie's asked Freddie and James and George. I've asked Priscilla Browne and Sallie Gardiner and now I'm asking you. Do say you'll come. Sallie Gardiner has often said it's not your fault your family has so little money, and I agree. You're quite the nicest girl in our class, and very ladylike in spite of your family's straits."

"Why, thank you," Meg said. "A picnic sounds lovely."

"It will be," said Mary. "We'll play games and eat ice cream and have the most wonderful time."

"I'll have to ask my mother first," Meg said. "But if she says I may, I'd love to attend your picnic."

"I'm so glad," Mary said. "Please tell your mother that my mother thinks she is the most splendid lady. Tell me tomorrow whether you can come. The picnic will be at one o'clock on Saturday. I do hope you'll attend." She took Meg's hand and gave it an affectionate squeeze, then walked away to join her brother, Willie.

Meg was so delighted, she laughed out loud with joy.

# Jo's Story

## CHAPTER 1

"Josephine! Josephine March!"

Jo March sighed and turned to face Aunt March. Only Aunt March called her Josephine, and only Aunt March used that tone of voice with her.

"Yes, Aunt March?" she asked.

"What is that book in your hand?"

"It's *Oliver Twist*, Aunt," Jo replied. "By Charles Dickens."

"I know who wrote *Oliver Twist*, young lady," said Aunt March. "That book came off my shelves, did it not?"

"Yes, Aunt March," Jo said. Aunt March's library was the best thing about visiting her great-aunt. Actually, Aunt March's library was the *only* thing Jo enjoyed about visiting her great-aunt. But visit she must, or so her parents said.

"*Oliver Twist* is not suitable reading matter for a child," proclaimed Aunt March. "Put it back on the shelves."

"But Father reads Dickens to us all the time," Jo said. "He's read us *David Copperfield* and *Little Dorrit* and *A Christmas Carol. The Pickwick Papers* is my favorite book of all. But I've never read *Oliver Twist,* and I've always wanted to. Please let me borrow it."

"Perhaps your father agrees with me that *Oliver Twist* is unsuitable for such a young girl," said Aunt March.

"I'm not so young," Jo said. "I'm ten already."

"And a rude young girl, at that," Aunt March declared. "I sometimes wonder what kind of manners your parents are teaching you."

"Father and Marmee are the best parents in the world," said Jo angrily. "Don't you speak against them."

"And don't you use that tone with me, young lady," Aunt March said. "Have your parents never taught you to respect your elders?"

"Of course they have," Jo said.

"Then the fault must lie with you and not them," said Aunt March.

Jo could have kicked herself. All she wanted was to get this visit over with as fast as she possibly could. That meant not quarreling with Aunt March. Jo had simply become so excited when she'd found the copy of *Oliver Twist*, she'd forgotten her mission of getting in and out in a half hour's time.

"I'm sorry, Aunt March," said Jo, and she was sorry—sorry she'd aroused Aunt March's wrath, since it meant she'd be there for at least another ten minutes and would probably go home without the precious Dickens volume to read.

"I will never understand why you can't be more like your sister Margaret," said Aunt March. "Now, there's a girl your parents can be proud of. She's every inch a lady."

"Yes, Aunt March," Jo said. She tried to hide the copy of *Oliver Twist* in the folds of her skirt. "Meg is a lady."

"You could learn something from your sister Beth as well," said Aunt March. "Quiet as a church mouse and never causing any trouble."

"Yes, Aunt March," Jo said.

"Even little Amy could teach you a thing or two," said Aunt March. "She is such a darling child. Not at all the sort of child who talks back."

"Yes, Aunt March," Jo said for what felt like the hundredth time. Of course Aunt March had a point. Meg was a lady—always polite, always willing to help others. Beth was a dear, sweet and kind—everyone loved her. Amy was pretty and artistic, and even if she drove Jo to distraction, she was the sort of child Aunt March would favor.

And Jo was just the sort of girl that Aunt March would want to improve. Jo was sharp-tongued, quick-tempered, and boyish.

"I suppose your parents have done as good a job as they could raising you girls, having so little money and so many ideals," Aunt March declared. "Your sisters, at least, are a credit to them."

"I'll try to be better," said Jo.

Aunt March shook her head. "I've heard you make that promise a hundred times before, Josephine."

"It's hard," Jo blurted out. "I'm not Meg and I'm not Beth and I'm not Amy. Goodness comes so easily to them. To Meg and Beth, at least. And people always forgive Amy her mistakes because of her blond curls and pretty ways."

"You might not have Amy's blond curls,"

said Aunt March, "but couldn't you learn from her pretty ways?"

Jo thought about it for a moment. "No," she said, "I don't think I could."

Aunt March stared at Jo, and then, much to Jo's surprise, she laughed out loud. "I suspect you're right," she said. "Very well. You've paid your old aunt her visit. You may go home now."

"Thank you, Aunt March," Jo said. She walked over to her aunt and gave her a kiss on the cheek.

"But give me back *Oliver Twist*," said Aunt March. "When I speak to your parents next, I'll ask them if they approve of it for you. If the answer is yes, you may borrow it the next time you visit me."

"Oh, thank you, Aunt," said Jo, knowing that was far better than she could have hoped for. And the visit was over. It was all she could do to keep from skipping out of her great-aunt's house as she escaped and turned toward home.

# Beth's Story

## CHAPTER 1

"I do believe," Father March said, looking at his wife and their four daughters as they finished eating their supper, "that this is my favorite part of the day."

"Mine too," his second-oldest daughter, Jo, said. "It means school is over and so are our tasks, and we can spend the evening however we want."

"I like the mornings best," said Amy, the youngest of the girls. "The light is better then for drawing. Of course, in February there's hardly any light at any time of day. I like mornings best in the summer."

"I like midafternoon the best," Meg, the oldest, said. "Even on a cold winter's day. It's the warmest time of the day, and the sun shines the brightest."

"What about you, Bethy?" Marmee asked. "What is your favorite time of day?"

"I don't have a favorite," Beth replied. "It would be like having a favorite sister. Each is wonderful in her own way. So is each time of day."

Marmee laughed. "I agree with Beth," she said. "Morning, noon, and night—they each have something to recommend them."

"And like your daughters, they each could stand a little improvement!" Jo said, and they all joined in her laughter.

"Nonetheless," Father said, "to sit here after one of Hannah's fine suppers, and to look at my wife and my four beautiful daughters—this is contentment of the purest kind."

"Notice how he puts supper first," Jo said. "Wife and daughters come after a full stomach."

"But the joy I get from my wife and daughters is a constant," replied her father. "And supper comes but once a day."

"He has you there, Jo," Meg said.

"But I fear this contentment will not last forever," said Father.

"Why not?" asked Beth, who was always fearful of change.

"He means we'll grow up," Meg said, "and marry and have families of our own." That was her dream.

"Not for a while, I should think," said Jo. "You're thirteen, Meg, and I'm twelve. I don't think Father approves of child brides."

"He said it wouldn't last forever," said Meg, "not that it was about to end next week."

"But next week is just when it will end," said Father.

His four daughters fell silent. Beth felt fear clutch her. Was Father going to leave? Where would he be going?

"Your father is teasing you," Marmee said. She reached out to give Beth's hand a reassuring pat. "We're going to take a trip, that's all."

"A trip?" Jo asked. "Where to? Are we all to come along?"

"Your mother and I are going to New York City," replied Father. "We'll take the train there next week and stay for a week."

"How exciting!" Meg exclaimed. "Will you shop while you're there? Marmee, I hear the stores in New York are almost equal to those in London and Paris."

"And they're every bit as expensive," said Marmee. "I'll look around for bargains, but I doubt I'll find any. However, that's not the reason for the trip."

"What is, then?" asked Amy.

"There are several reasons, actually," Father said. "As you girls know, there is fear of a possible war in this country. The Southern states want to continue the expansion of slavery, and of course many of us in the North want slavery abolished altogether. Several of my friends here have asked me to go to New

York to speak with some of the leading aboli-
tionists, Mr. Horace Greeley and the Rever-
end Henry Beecher, for example, to
determine what they think is likely to happen
and to find out what we and they can do in
the event of a war to see to it that slavery is
finally ended."

"Mr. Greeley and Mr. Beecher!" Meg said.
"They're both so famous. Do you know them,
Father?"

"I've met them both, yes," Father said.
"And we've exchanged letters recently. They
agree it's a good idea for us to speak. This is
an election year, and there are those who believe that if Mr. Lincoln is elected president,
civil war will follow."

"And a jolly good thing it would be," said
Jo. "I only wish I were a boy so I could fight
for the rights of the slaves."

"War is never a jolly good thing, Jo," her
father declared, "no matter how just the
cause. I pray that a peaceable solution will be
found, but I fear none will be."

"So you'll be speaking to Mr. Greeley, and Marmee will be looking for bargains," Meg said. "It still sounds like a wonderful trip."

"It's more wonderful than that," Marmee said. "We'll be staying with my friend Mrs. Webster. Her daughter, Catherine, is engaged to marry a gentleman named Mr. Kirke."

"Are you going for the wedding?" asked Meg.

"I'm going to help prepare the trousseau," Marmee replied. "And to visit with my old friend. Mrs. Webster owns a boardinghouse, so there will be plenty of room for us to stay."

"And you'll be gone for a whole week, Marmee?" Beth asked. She knew she should be happy for her parents to have such an exciting trip planned, but she already missed them.

"A week," said Father. "Hardly enough time for all that's planned."

"What else will you be doing?" asked Amy.

"We want to go to the theater," Marmee said. "Edwin Booth is playing in *Hamlet*. And

Mrs. Webster says we simply must see a production of *Uncle Tom's Cabin*. You know, the novel was written by Mr. Beecher's sister, Harriet Stowe. And what I think is most exciting of all, your father has agreed to have his photograph taken."

"Really?" Jo said.

"Mr. Emerson thinks it's a good idea," her father replied.

"And so do I," said Marmee. "I know I'll cherish a photograph of my handsome husband. And Mathew Brady, the most important photographer in this country, has consented to take the picture."

"What a week," said Meg. "The theater, politics, a trousseau, Mathew Brady, and shopping!"

"I never thought Meg would put shopping last on her list of pleasures," Jo said, and they all laughed, even Meg.

"But there's one other thing to make it more perfect," said Father. "Your mother and I have gone over the expenses for the trip several times, and we agree that if we're careful about how we spend our money, we can afford to take one of you along."

"A week in New York!" cried Jo. "Oh, take me, please."

"No, me," said Amy.

"I should love it also," Meg said. "And I love to sew. I could help with the trousseau."

Beth only smiled.

"We suspected you would all want to go," said Marmee. "So we've decided to let you girls choose who will get to spend a week in New York with us."

Beth looked at her sisters, all brimming with excitement. It would be a hard choice, but she knew whoever was selected would be the most deserving of the treat.

## ABOUT THE AUTHOR OF
## PORTRAITS OF LITTLE WOMEN

SUSAN BETH PFEFFER is the author of both middle-grade and young adult fiction. Her middle-grade novels include *Nobody's Daughter* and its companion, *Justice for Emily*. Her highly praised *The Year Without Michael* is an ALA Best Book for Young Adults, an ALA YALSA Best of the Best, and a *Publishers Weekly* Best Book of the Year. Her novels for young adults include *Twice Taken, Most Precious Blood, About David,* and *Family of Strangers*. Susan Beth Pfeffer lives in Middletown, New York.

# A WORD ABOUT
## LOUISA MAY ALCOTT

LOUISA MAY ALCOTT was born in 1832 in Germantown, Pennsylvania, and grew up in the Boston-Concord area of Massachusetts. She received her early education from her father, Bronson Alcott, a renowned educator and writer, who eventually left teaching to study philosophy. To supplement the family income, Louisa worked as a teacher, a household servant, and a seamstress, and she wrote stories as well as poems for newspapers and magazines. In 1868 she published the first volume of *Little Women*, a novel about four sisters growing up in a small New England town during the Civil War. The immediate success of *Little Women* made Louisa May Alcott a celebrated writer, and the novel remains one of today's best-loved books. Alcott wrote until her death in 1888.